YOU BE THE DETECTIVE

"Paid through funds from the
Scioto Area Community
Foundation, Inc."

Also by Marvin Miller:

YOU BE THE JURY
YOU BE THE JURY: COURTROOM II
YOU BE THE JURY: COURTROOM III
YOU BE THE JURY: COURTROOM IV

YOU BE THE THE DETECTIVE

Marvin Miller

Illustrated by Bob Roper

SCHOLASTIC INC.
New York Toronto London Auckland Sydney

ISBN 0-590-42731-8

Copyright © 1991 by Marvin Miller.
All rights reserved. Published by Scholastic Inc.,
730 Broadway, New York, NY 10003.

36 35 34 33 32 31 30 29 28 27 26 :   3/0

Printed in the U.S.A.   40

First Scholastic printing, January 1991

For Randy and Audrey

CONTENTS

YOU BE
THE
DETECTIVE

Welcome to Your New Job!

Welcome to the Bureau of Investigation. My name is Detective Alexander Riddle. As you know, this is my last day on the job. You will be my replacement.

I have been a detective here for ten years, ever since I got out of law school. It's a good place to work. Chief Anvil is a tough but fair boss. But I have decided that being a detective is not what I want to do in life, so I have decided to go back to school — to be an artist.

I am turning all my files over to you. As you will see, I do my best thinking with a pencil and a drawing pad in my hands. For every case, I have sketched a drawing of the scene of the crime. There are often clues at the scene of a crime that a sharp eye can detect. Take a good look at the drawing and read my report of the case.

At the end of each case you will find another drawing. This drawing shows my sketch that

1

solves the mystery. You will notice that I have cut this drawing into pieces and rearranged the pieces.

I have done this for two reasons.

First, you will have a chance to check my report and come to your own conclusion about the case. Then you can check your solution with mine by cutting out the puzzle pieces and putting my drawing back together again. (If you're having trouble putting the puzzle together, the number on the back of each piece will help you find the correct order. If you can't wait to do the puzzle, you can also find my written solution at the end of each case.)

Second, Chief Anvil is a puzzle fan. He loves putting together jigsaw puzzles. When I found this out, I decided to always give him the solutions to my cases as jigsaw puzzles. This way he could put them together for himself.

Well, I see it's getting late. Gosh, I'm going to miss this place. Here are my files. Good luck! I'm off to be an artist.

You be the detective!

The Case of
the Circus Footprints

On August 31, a worried man called my office at Headquarters. "The circus has been robbed," he said.

"My name is Richard Riley, and I am the owner of Riley's All-Star Circus," he said. "We have our big top pitched on the Higgins High School football field. Do you know it? This morning a cash box holding pay for my performers was stolen."

Suddenly childhood memories came rushing back to me. I had seen "Robust Richard" Riley doing his circus strongman act on my twelfth birthday. He was the strongest man I had ever seen. Now he'd been robbed.

"Last night, we finished the last performance of the summer," Riley continued. "I counted the money this morning. My ticket taker also counted. I hid the cash box in the ticket booth. When I returned from breakfast, it was gone."

I was on the scene in fourteen minutes flat.

I could see the bright red and green stripes of the big top from the parking lot. I could also see a row of circus trailers set up about twenty yards behind the tent. The field was surrounded by a high chain-link fence.

Riley met me at the gate — the only gate. With him was a man in a uniform.

"Detective Riddle! I'm so glad you are here," he said. "I'll show you where we had the money hidden."

Riley led me along a short sawdust path to the ticket booth. The sawdust felt like little pillows under my feet. I looked behind me. I made a footprint with every step.

The ticket booth had windows on three sides, including a big window in the door. The door was open, but no glass was broken. Except for a chair, the booth was completely empty.

"See the footprints?"

Riley's finger pointed to the side of the ticket booth. About two dozen footprints led from the ticket booth to the row of circus trailers. Another row of footprints led from the trailers to the booth. I also saw what looked like two palm prints.

I took my out my pad and pencil. I began to draw what I was seeing:

4

It was clear that these were the footprints of the thief who had walked from the trailers to the ticket booth and back again. Unknowingly the thief had left his footprints in the soft, freshly swept sawdust. But why were there also two palm prints? Had the thief fallen? Perhaps he had a bad leg.

I looked again at the footprints. They were small. A size five shoe, I guessed. The heel of each shoe had made a small, deep hole. Obviously they were high-heeled shoes. Now I imagined my thief differently. He was a she.

"I read in the newspaper that your ticket taker is also the ringmaster, or should I say ringmistress, of the circus," I said to Riley.

"Oh, you can't possibly suspect Tara!" he cried. "Miss Blossom is by far the most faithful member of our small circus. I cannot run the show without her," Riley protested. "Besides, she was with me at breakfast this morning."

"Have any of your performers injured their legs lately?" I asked him. I was thinking about the palm prints again.

"We are all in top shape," he said. "Not a single performer has needed to see a doctor all year. I am proud of that."

"Did you see anyone else up early this morning?" I asked. "Besides Miss Blossom?"

"Just Mr. Wilde, the animal trainer."

"What exactly was he doing?" I asked.

"He was sweeping the grounds. I saw him at about eight o'clock, just as Miss Blossom and I went out the gate to breakfast."

"Is this unusual for Mr. Wilde?"

"Not at all. His animals trample the path after every performance. He sweeps it smooth every morning," Riley said.

Whether or not Wilde had committed the crime, I already owed him a favor. His sweeping had provided me with the time of the crime. The footprints had been made sometime after eight o'clock this morning.

"Mr. Riley," I said. "Would you please make me a list of the shoe sizes of all your performers?"

Riley gave me a puzzled look. But then he nodded and left.

I returned my gaze to the thief's footprints. Then I followed them with my eyes. Where did they lead? Where did they come from?

They began and ended where the sawdust ended — at the raised wooden walkway. That walkway connected all of the trailers. All traces of footprints ended at the walkway.

I looked down the long row of trailers. Each trailer had a name painted on it. *Tara. Richard.*

Big George Wilde. Alexandra Loftwalker. Button the Clown. Bert Twirl.

Next to each name was a giant painting of the performer in action. I already knew who the first three were. Alexandra Loftwalker was a tightrope walker. She was shown balancing on one foot, high above a crowd. Button the Clown was shown with a pie being thrown in his face. Bert Twirl, the acrobat, was doing a handstand.

I had never had a list of suspects so large and brightly painted. I liked it.

"I found these," said a voice.

It was Riley, back again with the list. He was also holding up a pair of high-heeled shoes.

"They were behind the trailers," he said. The shoes were covered with sawdust, inside and out. "They are Tara's, if you must know," he said with a frown. "But she wasn't wearing them this morning. She was wearing her blue sneakers. I remember it well."

"Thank you," I said. "Thank you very much."

Here is the list of shoe sizes Riley gave me:

Tara Blossom (ticket taker): size 5.

Big George Wilde (animal trainer): size 10.

Alexandra Loftwalker (tightrope walker): size 7½.

Barry Buttonni (Button the Clown): size 8.

8

Bert Twirl (acrobat): size 9½.

Richard Riley (owner): size 12.

Only Blossom had the right shoe size. But she had been with Riley.

I looked at her shoes. I checked one against the thief's footprints. It fit perfectly.

It gave me an idea. Perhaps the thief had simply slipped Tara's two small shoes over the toes of his larger shoes. I decided to test the idea on a smooth area of sawdust. I expected success, of course. But after two steps, I fell hard. It didn't work.

The thief had needed only one hand to catch himself when he fell. I guess I didn't have the knack. The new footprints I had made with Tara's shoes looked different from the thief's footprints. I could even see the outline of my own shoe circling the outline of the smaller shoe. Someone with bigger feet couldn't possibly have put on Tara's shoes.

I sat down in disgust.

I looked at Riley's list again. I looked at my sketch. Palm prints. Two palm prints. What could it be? Then I noticed that the thief had fallen on one hand while going toward the ticket booth, and on the other hand while returning. Why? Perhaps this wasn't a case of a bad leg after all. I picked up my pencil, then my pad.

9

I began by drawing the scene of the crime. Then, for fun, on the next six pages, I drew each performer in the middle of his or her circus act. One of the drawings caught my eye.

Suddenly I had it! It was the only way. It made sense and it was easy.

To the criminal's portrait, I added a pair of red shoes and a brown shoulder bag with the cash box in it. At last, the solution was mine.

On my way out, I stopped at the gate. I told Riley who the thief was.

Then I borrowed a pair of scissors and cut my final drawing into little pieces. I knew that when Chief Anvil put this puzzle together, he'd flip.

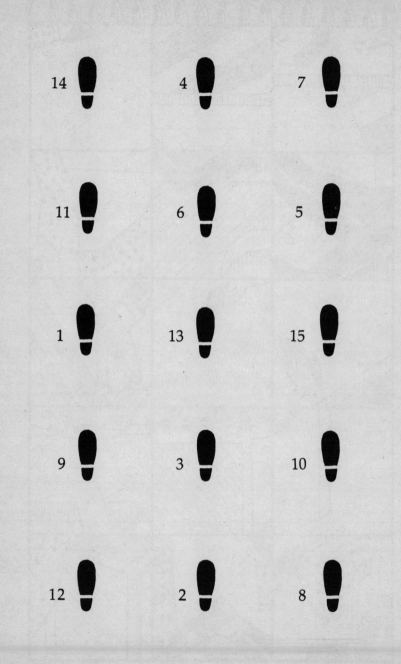

FINAL REPORT TO THE CHIEF

It was the palm prints that gave away Bert Twirl. None of the performers' feet could fit into Tara's shoes. But someone's *hands* could easily fit inside.

Only one person could have walked to the ticket booth with his hands in Tara's shoes — an acrobat!

But Bert's hands had slipped out of the shoes — twice. He caught his balance, leaving the palm prints behind.

— CASE CLOSED —

13

The Case of the Lost Lighthouse Keeper

On July 15, an unusual call shattered the late-night quiet of Headquarters. "It's a ship-to-shore call," the Bureau operator said. "Who will take it?"

I took the call.

"Hello, Riddle? This is Ensign Malcolm Newhouse of the Coast Guard," barked a crackly voice. "I'm calling from Seagull Strait. A cargo ship, the *Rhonda Sue*, ran aground tonight. What's left of her is hanging off Hopeless Rock. We have a real mess here, and we suspect that something has happened at the Seagull Point lighthouse. Can you help us out there?"

"Newhouse," I said, "why are you calling the Bureau of Investigation? Problems with lighthouses are taken care of by the Coast Guard. That's your job."

"We've called out all our crews to help clean up. We can't cover the lighthouse tonight." The hiss of static filled the phone for a moment. Then

Newhouse continued, "The captain of the *Rhonda Sue* missed the channel because the light never came on at Seagull Point lighthouse."

A shiver ran down my spine. Seagull Point lighthouse was one of the last nonautomatic lighthouses left in the country. Old Man Kettle had run the Seagull Point lighthouse since I was old enough to know what a lighthouse was. It was unthinkable that he would forget to turn it on.

I was on the scene in half an hour.

In the dark, the houses on Seagull Point Road looked eerie among the tall pines. I saw a light on in every house. Everyone was home.

As I turned left onto Lighthouse Road, the sight of the red and white "candy stripes" of the old lighthouse tower gave me a warm feeling inside. Seagull Point lighthouse itself looked as pretty as a postcard. Two small outdoor spotlights on the front lawn lit it up like a museum piece. But without its powerful beam, it looked dead.

I parked and yanked my evidence bag, a flashlight, and my sketch pad from the trunk. Then I climbed the stairs to the top room of the tower. I saw no one, but I did spot a large switch. It looked like something from the horror movie *Frankenstein*. It was turned to "Off." I quickly dusted for fingerprints. Then, after a moment's hesitation, I turned it on.

The powerful light that filled the round room made me squint. Soon the huge lens in the center began to revolve.

At least the Coast Guard has its light back again, I thought to myself. Satisfied for now, I descended the steep, twisting stairs.

The living quarters downstairs were deathly quiet. Usually the foghorn blared. But tonight, I could hear the waves outside. Old Man Kettle was nowhere to be found. What had happened to him?

Then I saw the note. It was scrawled on a chalkboard under the word *Weather*. The note read *Seagull Point lighthouse dark = Kettle safe*.

My heart sank. It looked like someone had kidnapped Old Man Kettle. The note on the chalkboard seemed to be a warning. It seemed to say that Kettle would be safe only as long as the lighthouse light was turned off.

I thought of the switch I had thrown. Had the kidnappers seen the light go back on? What would they do now?

I searched for the chalk used to write the note. But the house was empty of pens, pencils, or anything else to write with! I was puzzled.

I walked into the kitchen. It looked as if there had been a struggle. Two chairs were knocked over. Sugar had been spread across the table. The floor was wet with spilled coffee. A mug lay on its side on the floor. A box of sugar was still standing on the table.

The mug had just a trace of coffee left in it. Compared to the air in the room, the mug felt warm. That meant the crime had happened within the hour. The kidnappers were close — close enough to see the lighthouse light.

I sketched the scene. As I worked, the overhead light caught the surface of the table in a new way. Suddenly, there on the table, I saw something drawn into the spilled sugar:

But what could "337" possibly stand for? I remembered Kettle. He was no dummy. He may have been expecting trouble before it happened. The "337" was probably a clue that Kettle had written to who his kidnappers were. But what was it? Part of a telephone number? An address?

I called Headquarters. With a few reinforcements, I rounded up three suspects: Captain Morgan Helm, Bradford T. Shipworthy, and Lee Ron Tillerman. They all lived on Seagull Point Road, within plain sight of the lighthouse. As I interviewed them, two of my fellow detectives searched the suspects' houses for Kettle.

All three suspects looked tired and claimed to have been sleeping at the time of the crime. All had known Kettle for years, and claimed to have liked him. But each one also had a reason for wanting the Seagull Point light to go off.

One year ago, Morgan Helm had been the captain of the *Rhonda Sue*. Then, after months of poor health, he had lost his Coast Guard license. A man named Hogshead had taken his job on the *Rhonda Sue*.

Helm admitted that he and Hogshead were enemies. Helm said he had often wished that the *Rhonda Sue* and Hogshead would go down in a storm. But he added that he would never try to make such a thing happen.

Bradford Shipworthy was the owner of the small shipping company that owned the *Rhonda Sue*. Shipworthy's company had been losing money for two years. He said he had become depressed about it. Then a month ago, he took out a large insurance policy that would pay him for accidents at sea. If the *Rhonda Sue* sank, the insurance company would pay him a lot of money. But he said he had had nothing to do with causing this accident.

Of the three suspects, Lee Ron Tillerman knew Kettle best. By trade, he was a housepainter. He said he had painted the first red stripes on the Seagull Point lighthouse. For fifteen years, Tillerman and Kettle had played checkers together almost every day. But recently they had had an argument. Kettle thought that Tillerman was cheating at checkers, and Tillerman had gotten angry. Tillerman had called him "a cantankerous landlubber."

"I couldn't put up with that!" Tillerman said.

I asked the three in turn about the "337." Helm said he thought that the "337" was a code. "Kettle is an amateur cryptographer," he said. "Codes are his hobby."

Shipworthy and Tillerman offered no new ideas. All three also denied having written the note on the chalkboard.

After the interviews, I returned to my office with a sketch pad. I had to work fast. Kettle was still in danger.

The clue had to mean something. But what? The phone number idea seemed to lead nowhere. The local numbers all started with 609, not 337. Addresses in the area were only two digits long, not three.

I wrote out a simple alphanumeric code I remembered from seventh grade. We had used it to pass notes in the library. $1 = A$, $2 = B$, $3 = C$, $4 = D$, $5 = E$, $6 = F$, $7 = G$, etc., I wrote. Using this code, "337" might spell something. But "337" decoded into "CCG." Were those letters initials? None of the suspects had those initials.

If Kettle had known he was in trouble, he would have been smart not to hide the meaning of his clue too carefully.

Suddenly I had it. It was simple!

Quickly I redrew the scene of the crime with Kettle sitting at the table. Now Kettle's hasty message was as loud and clear as a buoy bell. I could see the solution clearly.

With one quick phone call I had my kidnapper before me in handcuffs. After hearing my evidence against him, he confessed and promised that the old lightkeeper was still within earshot of his beloved lighthouse, and safe.

21

After the police took the culprit away, I cut up my drawing and put it in the file. I knew that when Chief Anvil put this puzzle together, the solution would really leap out at him.

11

 4

 12

 13

 10

 3

 14

 7

 15

 2

 5

 9

 8

 1

 6

FINAL REPORT TO THE CHIEF

Kettle had sat on the *other side* of the table.
The kidnapper must have been with him.
Kettle suspected trouble. He spilled some sugar while fixing his coffee. Then he secretly wrote his kidnapper's first name in the sugar — LEE. Upside down, it looked like the number 337. Lee Ron Tillerman never knew it would tip off the Bureau.

— CASE CLOSED —

The Case of
the Edible Evidence

On November 3, I was hanging up my blue parka on the office coatrack when the owner of Frank's Fast Mart phoned Headquarters. He sounded upset.

"I had a break-in, Detective Riddle. I think it happened last night."

I hadn't even shaken the snow off my boots. Now I might not have to.

"They didn't steal money. They stole a handful of fruits and vegetables," he went on. "One carrot. Some cherries. And a few figs. That's about all. It's the strangest break-in I've ever seen. Can you come right over?"

I decided not to rush, considering the crime Frank had described. But even if it had been more serious, I still wouldn't have had to rush. I could be there in two minutes on foot, even over all those unshoveled sidewalks.

Frank's Fast Mart sits on the same block as Bureau headquarters. Four days out of five, I was there at noon to buy a turkey sandwich or my usual tuna on whole wheat with lettuce and tomato. I saw more of Frank than I saw of many of my best friends.

I put my coat back on and grabbed my pad.

When I arrived on the scene, Frank was waiting for me outside. "I haven't opened for business yet. I just can't tell how serious this is. Maybe this weirdo will come back."

I saw nothing wrong outside. The big glass windows looked a little steamed up, but they weren't broken. "Your heat is working," I said.

"I opened this lock myself this morning," Frank said. He was pointing to a heavy padlock hanging from a hasp on the opened door. The door was not damaged in any way.

We stepped inside and stamped our feet to get the snow off our boots. It felt good to get in out of the wind. "So how did the thief get in?" I asked. "A back door?"

"Yeah. It's over here," Frank said, pointing to a door behind the sandwich counter. The door seemed to open out into an alley.

"No one has ever tried to pry open a door on my store," Frank said. "But when I came in this morning, the back door was wide open."

"Was the store this warm when you arrived?"

"Almost," he said. "I've only been here ten minutes. I turned the heat up when I got here."

The crime must have happened this morning, not last night, I thought. The store would have been freezing if the door had been open to the outside for more than an hour or so.

"I may even have left the door unlocked myself last night," Frank said, shaking his head. "I just don't remember. I was in a rush to drive home before the big snow. You know, by two o'clock yesterday afternoon they were talking about closing schools today. So I closed up early."

"Do you remember shutting the door?"

"Oh, yes. The door was shut tight when I left."

"So let's see what the thief took," I suggested.

Frank led me down Aisle 1. First he showed me a bag of carrots. The bag was split open at the top. "One carrot is missing from this bag," Frank said. "One. Just one."

"Are you sure?" I asked.

"I buy carrots by the bag. They come seven to a bag. This one has six and a big hole."

He pointed further down the aisle. A bunch of cherries was spilled out across the floor.

"A handful of cherries is gone," Frank explained.

"Were the aisles clear last night before you left?"

"They were clean and clear, as usual. I always check the aisles before I leave," he said. We walked to the back of the store and turned into Aisle 2.

"A few figs," Frank said, holding up a torn cellophane package. "Not the whole package of figs, mind you — just a few. I mean, does that make sense? This guy wasn't very hungry."

I had to agree.

I told Frank to check his store one more time, top to bottom, and to call me if he found anything more valuable missing. I said I would talk to his neighbors, and give him a report as soon as I could.

"Today's tuna — right?" he said as I left.

I smiled. But I felt more puzzled than hungry.

Outside, I talked to two of Frank's neighbors.

They stopped shoveling just long enough to say they had seen nothing suspicious.

"Just all these kids out today," said one, ducking a volley of well-packed snowballs.

Nearby, a worker in a blue hard hat climbed down from a nearby telephone pole to answer questions. He said he had not seen a thing.

I crossed the street. Two kids were making a huge snowball from the snow on the library lawn. A sign in the library window read CLOSED TODAY. DEPOSIT RETURNED BOOKS BELOW. Wind had piled sticky snow right up and over the book deposit slot.

Two doors away was Diner 24, where I was certain I could find a witness. Diner 24 was named for the number of hours it was open each day. Only one other business on the street stayed open as many hours as Diner 24 did, and I worked for that place. So I knew Diner 24 well.

From two A.M. to ten, Donna Margonni sits at the cash register. She would have had a clear view of Frank's at the time of the crime.

"Not much business last night, Detective," she said. "Everyone must have gone home before the snow. It was quiet out there until the first plows came," she said. "Anyway, I guess I was more interested in watching the snow fall than in what was going on at Frank's."

I asked her to quiz her late-night customers anyway, when she saw them next. Then I headed back to Headquarters.

The next day was calm at work. The snow day must have temporarily put a damper on crime. It was sunny out and warm, with no wind. Much of the snow had melted. So I decided to take a stroll to Frank's to see if he had found anything more valuable than cherries missing.

"Nothing," he told me. "In fact, I found an extra two dollars on the counter after you left yesterday."

I ordered a turkey sandwich and a milk shake, to go.

As I left Frank's, I saw Donna in the window at Diner 24, so I stopped in again.

Donna's customers had no new leads for me.

"We have better milk shakes than Frank's," she said as I opened the door to leave. "You should know that, Detective Riddle."

On the way back to Headquarters, I passed the library again. Grass was showing through the melted snow. Suddenly I spotted something interesting: a carrot in a small patch of snow. Looking closer, I saw that the wide end of the carrot and the greens had been chopped off and were missing.

Less than a yard away, in a pool of water,

were eight cherry pits. Nearby lay a few un-eaten figs.

The stolen goods — but why here? And why would anyone steal them and only eat the cher-ries? This little case was beginning to amuse me.

I took out my pad and sketched the scene:

I studied my drawing for a while. Then I made a new drawing. Suddenly I had it.

Frank, Donna, and I had no weirdo burglar on our block. The thief had merely taken part in a harmless prank.

I quickly cut up my new drawing and stuck it in my sketch pad. I knew that when Chief Anvil saw this puzzle, he'd be really surprised. The solution to the crime was as plain as the nose on his face.

9   14   8

3   5   12

4   15   7

13   2   10

6   11   1

FINAL REPORT TO THE CHIEF

This case was a tough one. As I studied my first drawing, I got to thinking. Maybe the robber never meant to eat the carrot and figs.

I remembered the kids making the giant snowball. Then it hit me. They were making a *snowman!*

It had a carrot for a nose. The figs were used for eyes and buttons. The outline of a mouth was dotted with eight cherry pits.

When the kids discovered that Frank had left the back door to the Fast Mart unlocked, they had helped themselves, leaving the money on the counter to pay for what they'd taken.

If the sun hadn't melted the snowman, this case would have been a lot easier to solve.

— CASE CLOSED —

The Case of
the Haunted House

On October 31, a real estate agent called Headquarters from a pay phone on Lake Avenue. She
sounded out of breath.

"Detective, I need your help." Her voice qua-
vered as she spoke. "I've seen a ghost."

I suggested that she might have the wrong
number.

"I don't really think it's a ghost," she continued. "But the gardener at the house thinks it's
a ghost, and two different neighbors have seen
lights on at night in this house. It's supposed to
be empty." The caller identified herself as Alle-
gra Bramble, an agent for True View Realty.

I looked at my watch, then at my calendar. A
crime wave was sweeping a neighborhood on the
other side of town. I had no time for investigat-
ing Halloween pranks.

"Earl Browning hired me two months ago to
sell his family's hundred-year-old summerhouse,"
Bramble explained. "It's been empty for years.

They keep a gardener, so it won't look empty. But I'm certain that it isn't empty anymore."

"Ms. Bramble," I said. "I have seven burglaries on my hands in the Broadview area. Now if you think your situation deserves my immediate attention, then I'll come right over."

"I know it does," she said.

Forty minutes later, I pulled into a dirt-and-gravel driveway at 12 Lake Avenue. I was glad to get out of my car. Lake Avenue swerves along the shore of Glass Lake like a crazy mule. Sometimes it feels more like a BMX track than a quiet country road. The lake itself has so many inlets that most of the houses sit on their own private peninsulas. The old Browning house was one of these.

Bramble was sitting on the hood of her car.

"I've only been back inside the place once since I called you," she said. "I'm used to old houses, but this one gives me the creeps."

We walked toward its sagging old porch. Paint was peeling everywhere.

Bramble led me through a broken screen door to an old, musty living room. White sheets covered every piece of furniture. A large, old brass candlestick stood on the dusty mantel. Except for the floor, dust was everywhere.

"Who swept the floor?" I asked.

"Not me. This is exactly how I found the living room," Bramble said. "This is not the kind of house you sell by its cleanliness or the color of its paint, you know. We call this a handyman's special. The right buyer will be looking for the silver lining in this cloud of dust. In fact, the right buyer won't notice the dust at all."

"Why were you here today?" I asked.

"I came over to inspect the house," she said. "I do that with every house, before I show it."

Bramble then proceeded to tell me of her encounter with the ghost. More or less, this is how it went:

As Bramble walked through the living room, she began to hear noises. They came from a room near the back of the house. Arming herself with a candlestick, she investigated. She found the door to the room locked. But a skeleton key hanging on a nail nearby worked the lock. So she opened the door.

When her eyes adjusted to the darkness, she made out a white sheet — or a ghost. "It raised its arms like this," Bramble said, as she flapped her hands at her sides. "And it made an eerie sound."

Bramble was startled, but she didn't think she was in danger. It repeated the same movements over and over. "It looked as if it were trying to frighten me," Bramble said. "Then it lurched forward."

Bramble threw the candlestick at the ghost but missed. She slammed the door and locked it. Then she ran outside and called me from a pay phone.

Fifteen minutes later, she reentered the house. The noises were gone. The door was still locked. The key was still in the lock. When she unlocked the room, she found it empty.

While I had doubts about Bramble's story, I didn't think she was guilty of anything. I took her business card and said I would call her.

I started my inspection with the lock. It needed oil, but it worked. It also only worked from the outside. The "ghost" could not have unlocked the door from the inside and escaped.

I inspected the room itself. There was a narrow staircase and the single door that Bramble had opened. The walls were paneled with narrow pieces of dark wood.

The candlestick Bramble had thrown lay on the floor. I looked for a mark on the wall. Sure enough, a large gouge had been taken out of the paneling where the candlestick had hit the wall. I could see the mark from the doorway, where Bramble had stood when she threw.

But something was wrong. The candlestick lay

off to the side, several strides away from that mark. How could it have landed there? It should have been just below the mark. Its shape made it impossible to roll.

Then I examined the stairs. They led to a sleeping loft. They were thick with dust. There were no footprints in the dust. I glanced back around me at the four walls, looking for a window, but there was none.

I took out my sketch pad and made a record of the scene:

As I worked, I wondered if Bramble had made up this strange story. But I couldn't think of a reason why she would lie. The door was locked and there were no footprints on the stairs. How could anyone have disappeared from a locked room without leaving a trace?

As I finished drawing the candlestick in position, I put my pencil down. I decided to try an experiment.

I took the matching candlestick from the mantel in the living room. Then I stood in the doorway, as Bramble said she had done. With a good windup, I pitched the heavy candlestick overhand at the wall. It chipped the wood panel, and then fell to the floor where it came to an instant stop. It did not roll.

I tried again. And again. And again. After six throws, my candlestick had not once fallen anywhere near the first candlestick.

There was something odd about this whole case. I picked up my pad again, puzzled. I doodled and sketched. The longer I sketched, the more I relaxed. I sat down and leaned back. I closed my eyes.

With my eyes closed, a new image came to me. For some reason, I imagined the cat burglar that was plaguing the Broadview area. Would he be prowling again tonight? I wondered.

I tore the old sketches off my pad. On a new sheet of paper, I drew the burglar. He carried a large, black bag full of stolen valuables. Where would he take these things?

A successful burglar needs a safe place to hide. Could the Browning house be a hideout? No one lived here. It was also far from the crimes committed. No one would suspect it! If people thought the house was haunted, no one would want to buy it, and people would stay away.

These were all good ideas, but I had no proof. I went back to drawing.

First, I drew the room with the wood paneling. Then I added the candlestick flying through the air and bouncing off the wall. I drew the candlestick again on the floor where it should have landed.

I was on to something. But it didn't answer the questions of the candlestick and the escape from the locked room.

I leaned forward to draw. But this time, when I put my pencil back on paper, the simple answer to both of my questions swung out at me. Of course! It was the only way.

With a little help from Headquarters, I found my "ghost" within the hour. I had also solved the seven Broadview area burglaries and recovered the stolen property.

I cut up my new drawing and put it in my sketch pad. I had a feeling that when Chief Anvil worked on this puzzle, he'd see that this was an open-and-shut case.

15 6 3

1 7 13

9 8 14

2 5 4

11 10 12

FINAL REPORT TO THE CHIEF

My hunch was right. The Browning house was the burglar's hideout. He used it to store the stolen valuables.

Who would have thought a hundred-year-old summerhouse would have a secret door built into a wall panel?

When Bramble threw the candlestick, it bounced off the wall and fell right where it should have. After she locked the door and ran outside, the burglar escaped through the secret door.

As the hidden door swung open, it pushed the candlestick off to the side. That's exactly where I found it.

— CASE CLOSED —

The Case of
the Missing Money

On December 19, the president of a big chemical factory in town called me at Headquarters.

"Detective Riddle, someone has emptied the company safe. All the holiday bonus money for our employees is gone."

I held the phone away from my ear. Robert Gladstone, president of the We Care Chemical Company, seemed to enjoy shouting into the phone.

"I personally checked the safe last night before I left work. It was securely locked. This morning, I unlocked it. It was empty."

I told Gladstone I would be right over.

Before I left, I phoned for some help from the fingerprint lab. If I were lucky, the thief had left at least one clear fingerprint inside the safe.

Half an hour later, I was on the scene.

The We Care Chemical Company sprawls over thirteen acres of hilly ground at the edge of town. From the main entrance gate, fields of brightly painted chemical drums and dull gray buildings stretch almost as far as the eye can see.

Robert Gladstone met us inside the main building and led us straight to the safe. It was gigantic. Its shiny round door alone must have weighed 1,000 pounds. The open door was almost big enough to walk through. After a quick look around, I turned the safe over to the fingerprint crew. Gladstone pulled me over to a corner of the room.

"I personally withdrew an enormous amount of cash from our account at the bank yesterday," he boomed at me. "I put it in the safe myself. It looks like I was the last honest person to see it."

After a few quick sketches of the safe room, I drove home.

The next morning, fingerprints collected from the We Care Chemical Company safe were on my desk. Two sets of fingerprints were identified: Gladstone's and those of a janitor named Wilbert Fitzwinkle.

I ran a background check on Fitzwinkle, and to my surprise, found that we had a file on him twenty pages long. Among his many crimes were four convictions for safecracking.

That night, we arrested Wilbert Fitzwinkle as he and his wife left the company party. Back at Headquarters I read him the file and he confessed.

But he refused to tell me where he had hidden the money. A week passed. Still he refused.

In desperation, I decided to follow his wife to see if she was suddenly spending a lot of money. Maybe she would lead me to where the money was hidden.

But Betty Fitzwinkle appeared to be out of money. I watched at the bank as she asked for a loan and was turned down.

An envelope from the phone company came to her with the words YOUR PAYMENT IS LATE in big red letters on the outside. A day later, I observed her buying a coat from a used clothing shop.

It was clear she didn't know where the money was.

Finally, the day before the trial, Betty Fitzwinkle gave us a break. While visiting her husband in jail, she begged him for money to buy groceries. The guard assigned to Fitzwinkle overheard their conversation.

"Bring me my gray-striped jacket for the trial tomorrow," Fitzwinkle told her. "And don't forget to sew the torn lining." According to the guard, Fitzwinkle repeated these instructions three times.

Mrs. Fitzwinkle finally had to borrow money from the guard. While she headed for the grocery store, I drove to the Fitzwinkles' apartment. Why had Fitzwinkle asked his wife three times to sew the lining of his jacket? I suspected that he had hidden something, maybe a map showing where the money was hidden, in the lining of his coat.

I opened the door to the Fitzwinkles' apartment with the key that Wilbert Fitzwinkle had turned over to the Bureau when he was arrested. It took me ten minutes to find the gray-striped coat hanging in the back of a hallway closet. Sure enough, the lining was torn.

I slipped my hand behind the lining. I found nothing.

Quickly I searched all the pockets. They were empty. I knew there had to be a secret hidden somewhere in the coat, but I was getting nowhere fast.

Maybe the map wasn't on a piece of paper at all. Maybe it had been written or sewn into the cloth. I turned the jacket inside out and inspected every fold and seam, but I still had no luck.

There was only one thing left to do. Using a

pair of Betty Fitzwinkle's sewing scissors, I cut the coat apart, piece by piece. I pulled out every pocket, every thread. But I still found nothing: no money, no map, no nothing.

Finally I got up, collected the pieces of the coat, locked the door, and drove home feeling foolish. It was clear to me now that Wilbert Fitzwinkle had meant nothing mysterious when he had asked his wife to sew the lining of his coat.

At home, I made myself some dinner.

But I couldn't eat. My mind was spinning.

I sat down in a chair and took out my drawing pad. I sketched the scene at the Fitzwinkles' apartment — the pieces of the gray-striped jacket lying on the table, Betty Fitzwinkle's sewing basket sitting nearby, full of thimbles, needles, and spools of different-colored thread. It looked like this:

Drawing a picture made me feel calmer, as it always does. But something didn't seem right.

I thought about what Fitzwinkle had been wearing. We had arrested him in a brand-new brown plaid suit with matching trousers. But the coat he'd asked his wife to bring for the trial was gray-striped. Why would he want to wear a striped coat that wouldn't match his pants? I began to think that my first idea about the importance of the jacket was not so far off after all.

I tried to imagine myself in Betty Fitzwinkle's shoes, trying desperately to make sense of her husband's instructions. Fitzwinkle would want to look as sharp as possible for the trial. Why then ask for his old, torn coat? I imagined Betty Fitzwinkle reaching for a needle and thread. I started drawing again.

Suddenly I had it. Simple!

I quickly called the Bureau. "Send an officer to the Fitzwinkle apartment right away," I said. "And follow these instructions. . . . "

In less than ten minutes an officer had found the map that showed us where the money was hidden.

While I waited at home, I cut up my final drawing and put it in the case file on my desk. I could hardly wait for the look on Chief Anvil's face when he saw how I'd unraveled this mystery.

3 10   9

7 6   12

1   15   13

5 8 2

14   11 4

FINAL REPORT
TO THE CHIEF

If Betty Fitzwinkle had sewn her husband's jacket, she would have found the hidden map. Wilbert Fitzwinkle was very clever. He had unwound some gray thread from its spool. Then he wrapped the map around the next layer and rewound the thread over it.

I had handled the gray thread and had never even known I was holding the map that would lead us to Fitzwinkle's stolen money!

— CASE CLOSED —

The Case of
the Stolen Trees

Just before dark on December 22, my phone rang at Headquarters.

"Detective Riddle?" said a woman's voice when I answered the phone. "I would like to alert you to a crime in progress at Paisley Park. A man in overalls has parked his blue pickup truck in a corner of the park. He has what looks to be a large handsaw. As we speak, he is cutting down yet another tree. These trees are city property. As a good citizen, I must question this activity. It looks very suspicious."

"I understand," I said.

"Now will you come arrest him? Or shall I take the law into my own hands?" she asked.

I glanced at my watch. This seemed to be a case for the Parks Department. But I had planned to have dinner downtown anyway.

"I'll be there right away, Ms. . . ."

"Mrs. Hortensia H. Buffington. I live at Paisley Manor Hotel, 333 North Avenue, sixth floor."

Ten minutes later, I pulled into the circular drive of the Paisley Manor Hotel. As I stopped, a doorman opened the back door of my car, and an elderly woman slid into the backseat.

"Turn left there," she said before the doorman had closed the car door. "This shortcut will bring us directly to the scene of the crime."

We drove into Paisley Park. A minute later she held up her hand and told me to stop.

Our short walk to the scene of the crime took less than a minute. Pine needles were everywhere. About a dozen fresh stumps cut at odd angles rose out of the ground. The smell of pine sap filled the air.

"Those trees had already reached twelve to fifteen feet in height, Detective," said Mrs. Buffington. "I remember the day the Friends of Paisley Park planted them — proud Scotch pines, every one. This thief should replace the trees with saplings and tend them until we can no longer tell that any damage occurred. I'd say he deserves at least seven years in the public service."

"Mrs. Buffington," I said. "Scotch pines are sold as Christmas trees, are they not?"

"They are the best Christmas trees, in my experience, Detective Riddle. And as you might guess, I have seen more than a few Christmasses."

"Can you describe the man you saw?"

"I saw overalls and a large handsaw, but it

61

was already so dark when I called you. He was medium height, I suppose. But I couldn't be certain."

"And the truck?"

She pulled a piece of paper from her handbag. "Here, Detective, is my sketch of the truck. I could not, of course, read the license plate number. But with my late husband's field glasses, I could make out the white sign on the side of the truck. It read BETTER CHICKEN FARMS. I'm quite certain of that."

When we returned to the hotel, I called Headquarters. "Tell everyone to watch for a blue pickup truck with a white sign on the door," I said.

I thanked Mrs. Buffington for her help and good citizenship and promised to let her know when I had solved the case.

That evening, I found the address for Better Chicken Farms in the phone directory. I drove out the next morning. All but one of their pickup trucks were red.

"Yes, sir, we're painting the fleet red," Perkin Peck explained. "We think that it will help people 'think chicken.' You know what I mean? White just didn't do the job. Hard to keep clean, too."

Peck, the owner of Better Chicken Farms,

said that he had not owned a blue pickup since 1969. I told him that someone driving a truck with his sign painted on the door was seen stealing trees.

"Naah. I can't believe it. This lady who saw it, how were her eyes?" said Peck.

Back at Headquarters, I found reports on dozens of blue pickups that had been spotted. But not one had a painted sign. There didn't seem to be a truck in town that matched Mrs. Buffington's description.

I decided to drive back to Better Chicken Farms to ask some more questions. A half hour later, I was back in my car, heading out of town. Suddenly I saw a farm with the sign: CHRISTMAS TREES FOR SALE. ALL SIZES STILL AVAILABLE. I pulled in.

"Selling trees?" I asked.

"Trying to," said the farmer who came out to meet me. "But nobody's buying. Want to be the first?" He introduced himself as Herb Flit, "Corn farmer for forty years, tree farmer for ten years, and grandfather for five."

"Do you raise chickens, too?" I asked.

"Chickens? No," Flit said. "You can find chickens in that direction," he said. "Better Chicken Farms. Just follow your nose."

I looked at the stacks of trees for sale in the

snow. They looked tall enough to be from Paisley Park. "Any Scotch pines?" I asked.

"Oh, yes. I have a few fifteen feet tall. Some say Scotch pines are the best. But some don't, so I have Douglas firs, too, but not so tall."

He said he hadn't been downtown in weeks.

Then I noticed the blue pickup truck half hidden by a fence near Flit's barn. I asked him if I could have a look.

The truck matched Mrs. Buffington's description almost perfectly: a blue pickup with a white sign on the door. The truck bed was full of pine needles. But the sign on the door did not match Mrs. B.'s description. It read FLIT FARM, not BETTER CHICKEN FARMS. I scratched my ear.

Could Flit have disguised his truck with a Better Chicken Farms sign and then painted over it afterward? I took a closer look at the sign. I felt each letter carefully with my fingers. Flit had not repainted the sign recently. The fading, pockmarked letters were as old as the truck.

Everything fit so perfectly — except for the sign. I took out my drawing pad and sketched the truck and sign quickly:

I thanked Flit for his help. On the way out, I counted his Scotch pines.

"Thirteen," said a voice. I spun around. There was no one there.

"Thirteen Christmas trees," said the voice. I looked down. Flit's five-year-old grandson was standing there, drawing numbers on a small chalkboard in his hand.

"I can count to thirteen," he said. "Want to hear me?" I listened to him twice. Then I showed him how to draw a tree.

Half an hour later, I drove into Paisley Park to count stumps: thirteen again.

How did Flit do it? Suddenly I remembered Christmas. Christmas! If only crime stopped on holidays.

I looked at the scene before me. I was pretty sure that Flit was the thief. Thirteen Scotch pines had been cut down, and he was selling thirteen Scotch pines.

The thief had driven a blue pickup truck with a white sign, and Flit owned a blue pickup with a white sign.

The only thing I couldn't figure out was the sign itself. Mrs. Buffington said that the thief's truck clearly read BETTER CHICKEN FARMS on the side, but the sign on Flit's truck had not been repainted.

7 11 15

14 10 12

9 5 1

3 6 2

13 4 8

I took out my drawing pad and began to doodle. First I drew the truck again. Then the sign. I continued to draw.

I found myself wondering what Flit would give his grandchild for Christmas. Maybe a toy pickup truck. The kid seemed to have artistic talent, too. Maybe Flit would give him a new chalk set or . . .

Suddenly I had it. I looked at my drawing. Could it be?

I drove to Paisley Manor Hotel and phoned Headquarters. I also left a quick note for Mrs. Buffington as I'd promised. Then I headed out to Flit Farm to arrest Herb Flit. I remembered Mrs. Buffington's suggestion for punishing the tree thief. I felt the punishment fit the crime.

When I got home that night I cut up my last drawing and placed it in the file. When Chief Anvil put this puzzle together, I knew he'd see that I had filled in all the details.

FINAL REPORT
TO THE CHIEF

I really should thank Flit's five-year-old grandson for helping me solve this one.

Now I know why Flit's sign was as old as his truck. He never painted *over* it. He *added to* it!

Flit had added chalk lines to the letters of FLIT FARM. The sign became BETTER CHICKEN FARMS.

After he stole the trees, Flit erased the evidence.

— CASE CLOSED —

The Case of
the Morning Monsters

Early one Friday morning, an elderly neighbor of mine called me. As I picked up the phone the sun was just breaking through the fog.

"Alexander, this is Peter Ploop. We're out of our wits today. Chester, Maggie, and I went to rescue a kitten and came face-to-face with a monster. We need your help."

I struggled not to laugh. Peter Ploop, Chester Fester, and Maggie Clickbeetle had been out of their minds for at least seventy years. This had nothing to do with age. They'd been wacky class clowns ever since they'd met each other in kindergarten. They were still best friends after all these years.

"The poor kitten," Peter continued. "Her careless master shut her up in a shed. Can you imagine?

"But when we tried to save her, we couldn't get near her. She's guarded by a monster! You must come help us at once. We'll meet you at Maggie's."

My experience with these three told me not to ignore their strange request. Peter, Chester, and Maggie had already cooked up more than their share of neighborhood mischief this spring. I put on a sweater and grabbed my pad.

"Sit down," Maggie said when I arrived, offering me a pink rocking chair. As usual, she was a sight in her long black cape. Her hairdo looked like a big black tornado turned upside-down. I couldn't decide if she looked more like the bride of Frankenstein or a woman with a beehive on her head.

"I have an hour," I said.

"Now what's the rush, Alexander?" said Peter. Peter Ploop had once been a college professor. No matter what the weather, Peter always dressed in a tweed jacket. He had a pointy pipe in his mouth, even though he didn't smoke. And because he thought it made him look distinguished, Peter carried a walking stick.

"We walked together early this morning," began Maggie, "as we do every morning, at daybreak. But today, we heard a kitten mewing loudly somewhere in the fog. The pitiful sound seemed to be coming from the new lot at the corner. It has a fence around it. Do you know it?"

I nodded.

"I simply could not walk by without trying to help," Maggie continued. "So I asked my two friends here to wait for me. And then I marched straight into the yard to do my good deed."

"Piles of lumber were everywhere," added Peter. "She could have tripped in the fog. She shouldn't have gone."

"But I did," said Maggie, glaring. "The sounds were coming from a large toolshed."

"She saw a monster!" Chester burst in.

"I did not," Maggie said, stamping her foot. "There was very little light inside the shed, but I could just make out the shapes of tools, boards, a large piece of equipment covered with a drop

cloth, a kitten — and hovering over it, the outline of a monstrous bird. It had huge dark wings
and a pointed head! As I moved toward the kitty
to rescue it, the bird spread its wings."

"She saw a monster!" Chester said again, slap-
ping the knee patches on his baggy pants.

Of the three, Chester dressed the most
plainly — but his clothes always looked four sizes
too big. Today, he had rolled up the sleeves of
his trench coat above his elbows and turned the
collar up. The long points of this overstarched
coat collar looked like two soldiers standing at
attention on opposite sides of a steep hill.

Chester continued, "Maggie wouldn't change
her story, so Peter offered to go rescue the
kitten. But he came back as white as a sheet!"

"The kitten was there, all right," Peter began.
"I also saw the tools and the drop cloth and all.
But I saw nothing like a bird. The strange creature that I saw had the head of a rhinoceros. I
saw its outline very clearly. But only its head
was animal! As I raised my arm to protect
myself, it pointed a stick at me. Then it attacked
me."

"So it was Chester's turn to rescue the kitten,"
Maggie said.

"I didn't believe a word from these two, Alexander. Truly I didn't," Chester began. "I thought

they had turned one of our little pranks on its head. But no! I saw the kitten, yes, and a drop cloth and some tools. But no bird or rhino. The outline I saw had two sharp horns — like a bull! It moved, but not in a threatening way. I myself am not afraid of bulls, so I was perfectly relaxed."

"Chester was so 'relaxed,' he ran right by us," Maggie added, laughing. "And he didn't stop running until he got back here."

"Shall we visit the shed now?" I asked.

"If we must," Maggie said, disappointed. "We were hoping you would pick the truth from our stories just by the telling of them."

"A good detective must trust his own eyes," Peter said.

"No," I said, changing my mind. "No, I'll accept your challenge. I will solve this strange case without visiting the scene. But you three have to promise me one thing."

"Name it," said Peter.

"Promise to give up your pranks for the summer," I said firmly.

"No pranks?" cried Maggie. "Oh, dear."

"I think that's fair," said Peter.

"But you must also free the kitten," Chester added somewhat anxiously.

"I will free the kitten. But I must draw a

while. Can the kitten survive fifteen minutes more?"

Maggie nodded thoughtfully.

I moved to Maggie's porch so I could be alone. I took out my drawing pad. I sketched my troublesome trio, just as they had appeared before me:

Then I sat back and thought about the stories I had just heard.

First, each witness had seen the kitten, so their stories agreed on at least one point. Next, everyone had seen tools and something covered by a drop cloth.

That gave me an idea. Could the equipment under the drop cloth have looked like a monster? No. All three said they had seen the monster move. But wait! Had everyone seen the creature clearly? No, they hadn't! In fact, one saw a bird, one saw a rhino, and one saw a bull. And hadn't they said it was foggy outside and very little light had entered the shed? Everyone had used the word "outline." Not one of them had seen the monster in any great detail.

I though some more. I imagined my neighbors coming face-to-face with their monster. ... .

Then I began a new drawing. It was of Maggie Clickbeetle being attacked by a monster bird. Suddenly I saw it all clearly. I had the solution!

I cut up my drawing and put it in my sketch pad. When Chief Anvil looked into this puzzle, and paused to reflect on how I'd solved this case, he'd know that I had been a good detective.

After slipping a quick note under Maggie's front door, I headed off to rescue the stray kitten. I thought I just might keep it.

FINAL REPORT TO THE CHIEF

I drew a picture of Maggie Clickbeetle coming face-to-face with a monstrous bird. Suddenly I knew there could be only one solution.

There was a big mirror inside the darkened toolshed!

Maggie had been looking at an outline of *herself*. The bird's pointed head was Maggie's funny hairdo. And its wings were her long cape.

Chester had never seen a sharp-horned bull. It was the points of his coat collar that stuck out on each side of his head.

And as for Peter, the pointy pipe in his mouth made his reflection look exactly like a rhinoceros. Peter was embarrassed when I told him that he had attacked himself with his own cane.

— CASE CLOSED —

NOTES

NOTES

NOTES